What Kids Say About Carole Marsh Mysteries . . .

"I love the real locations! Reading the book always makes me want to go and visit them all on our next family vacation. My Mom says maybe, but I can't wait!"

"One day, I want to be a real kid in one of Ms. Marsh's mystery books. I think it would be fun, and I think I am a real character anyway. I filled out the application and sent it in and am keeping my fingers crossed!"

"History was not my favorite subject till I starting reading Carole Marsh Mysteries. Ms. Marsh really brings history to life. Also, she leaves room for the scary and fun."

"I think Christina is so smart and brave. She is lucky to be in the mystery books because she gets to go to a lot of places. I always wonder just how much of the book is true and what is made up. Trying to figure that out is fun!"

"Grant is cool and funny! He makes me laugh a lot!!"

"I like that there are boys and girls in the story of different ages. Some mysteries I outgrow, but I can always find a favorite character to identify with in these books."

"They are scary, but not too scary. They are funny. I learn a lot. There is always food which makes me hungry. I feel like I am there."

What Parents and Teachers Say About Carole Marsh Mysteries . . .

"I think kids love these books because they have such a wealth of detail. I know I learn a lot reading them! It's an engaging way to look at the history of any place or event. I always say I'm only going to read one chapter to the kids, but that never happens—it's always two or three, at least!"
—Librarian

"Reading the mystery and going on the field trip—Scavenger Hunt in hand—was the most fun our class ever had! It really brought the place and its history to life. They loved the real kids characters and all the humor. I loved seeing them learn that reading is an experience to enjoy!"
—4th grade teacher

"Carole Marsh is really on to something with these unique mysteries. They are so clever; kids want to read them all. The Teacher's Guides are chock full of activities, recipes, and additional fascinating information. My kids thought I was an expert on the subject—and with this tool, I felt like it!"
—3rd grade teacher

"My students loved writing their own Real Kids/Real Places mystery book! Ms. Marsh's reproducible guidelines are a real jewel. They learned about copyright and more & ended up with their own book they were so proud of!"
—Reading/Writing Teacher

"The kids seem very realistic—my children seemed to relate to the characters. Also, it is educational by expanding their knowledge about the famous places in the books."

"They are what children like: mysteries and adventures with children they can relate to."

"Encourages reading for pleasure."

"This series is great. It can be used for reluctant readers, and as a history supplement."

The Mystery in
Icy
Antarctica

The Frozen Continent

by Carole Marsh

First Edition ©2008 Carole Marsh/Gallopade International/Peachtree City, GA
Current Edition ©2013
Ebook Edition ©2011
All rights reserved.
Manufactured in Peachtree City, GA

Carole Marsh Mysteries™ and its skull colophon are the property of
Carole Marsh and Gallopade International.

Published by Gallopade International/Carole Marsh Books. Printed in the United
States of America.

Managing Editor: Sherry Moss
Senior Editor: Janice Baker
Assistant Editor: Fran Kramer
Cover Design: Vicki DeJoy
Cover Photo Credits: ©Alexander Hafemann, istockphoto;
©Jupiterimages Corporation
Content Design and Illustrations: Janice Benight

Gallopade International is introducing SAT words that kids need to know in
each new book we publish. The SAT words are bold in the story. Look for
this special logo beside each word in the glossary.
Happy Learning!

Gallopade is proud to be a member and supporter of these educational organizations
and associations:

American Booksellers Association
American Library Association
International Reading Association
National Association for Gifted Children
The National School Supply and Equipment Association
The National Council for the Social Studies
Museum Store Association
Association of Partners for Public Lands
Association of Booksellers for Children

30 Years Ago . . .

As a mother and an author, one of the fondest periods of my life was when I decided to write mystery books for children. At this time (1979), kids were pretty much glued to the TV, something parents and teachers complained about the same way they do about web surfing and video games today.

I decided to set each mystery in a real place—a place kids could go and visit for themselves after reading the book. And I also used real children as characters. Usually a couple of my own children served as characters, and I had no trouble recruiting kids from the book's location to also be characters.

Also, I wanted all the kids—boys and girls of all ages—to participate in solving the mystery. And, I wanted kids to learn something as they read. Something about the history of the location. And, I wanted the stories to be funny. That formula of real+scary+smart+fun served me well.

I love getting letters from teachers and parents who say they read the book with their class or child, then visited the historic site and saw all the places in the mystery for themselves. What's so great about that? What's great is that you and your children have an experience that bonds you together forever. Something you shared. Something you both cared about at the time. Something that crossed all age levels—a good story, a good scare, a good laugh!

30 years later,
Carole Marsh

Hey, kids! As you see—here we are ready to embark on another of our exciting Carole Marsh Mystery adventures! You know, in "real life," I keep very close tabs on Christina, Grant, and their friends when we travel. However, in the mystery books, they always seem to slip away from Papa and me so that they can try to solve the mystery on their own!

I hope you will go to www.carolemarshmysteries.com and apply to be a character in a future mystery book! Well, the *Mystery Girl* is all tuned up and ready for "take-off!"

Gotta go...Papa says so! Wonder what I've forgotten this time?

Happy "Armchair Travel" Reading,

Mimi

About the Characters

 **Christina**, age 10: Mysterious things really do happen to her! Hobbies: soccer, Girl Scouts, anything crafty, hanging out with Mimi, and going on new adventures.

 **Grant**, age 7: Always manages to fall off boats, back into cactuses, and find strange clues—even in real life! Hobbies: camping, baseball, computer games, math, and hanging out with Papa.

 **Mimi** is Carole Marsh, children's book author and creator of Carole Marsh Mysteries, Around the World in 80 Mysteries, Three Amigos Mysteries, Baby's First Mysteries, and many others.

 **Papa** is Bob Longmeyer, the author's real-life husband, who really does wear a tuxedo, cowboy boots and hat, fly an airplane, captain a boat, speak in a booming voice, and laugh a lot!

Travel around the world with Christina and Grant as they visit famous places in 80 countries, and experience the mysterious happenings that always seem to follow them!

Books in This Series

Table of Contents

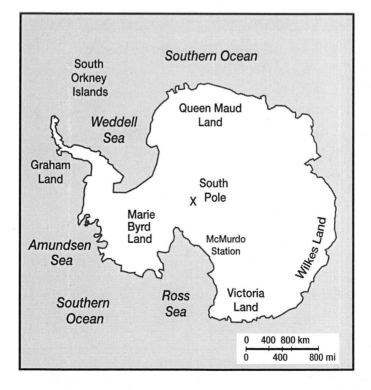

Antarctica

South Orkney Islands

Southern Ocean

Queen Maud Land

Weddell Sea

Graham Land

South Pole
X

Marie Byrd Land

McMurdo Station

Wilkes Land

Amundsen Sea

Ross Sea

Victoria Land

Southern Ocean

0	400	800 km
0	400	800 mi

Coming in on a Prayer and an Ice Floe

"Penguins! I can see penguins!" Grant shouted. His grandfather, Papa, banked their little red-and-white plane, the *Mystery Girl*, into position for landing. They were headed for the sea-ice landing field near McMurdo Station, Antarctica.

Christina, Grant's sister, stared at the bleak landscape below. "Nothing but miles and miles of ice and snow in every possible shade of blue and white!" she cried. She couldn't believe they were flying above the South Pole, and the coldest continent on earth! She and Grant often traveled with their grandparents. Their

grandmother, Mimi, wrote mystery books for kids, and traveled around the world to do research. This is definitely the "coolest" location we've been to, Christina thought.

Looking to the right, she saw the first signs of human life. "That must be McMurdo Station!" she said. "From here it looks so tiny and sad! Just drab tan buildings! And those spooky, black hills behind the station give me the shivers."

Mimi stared at the outside temperature gage. "Five degrees Fahrenheit! THAT gives me the SHIVERS," she moaned.

Papa was checking off descent procedures when a radio call interrupted him.

"*Mystery Girl*," the voice said, "McMurdo Station calling. You can't land now! Penguins are on the landing strip. We will notify you when the airfield is bird-free."

"Roger that," Papa replied.

The voice over the radio added, "For now, land on the ice floe on your left. It will take a while to remove the penguins. No use burning expensive fuel circling around."

2

Papa eyed the massive, free-floating ice floe that was now to be his runway. "Here goes a first," he said, grinning. "Tighten your seatbelts and hang on!"

"They certainly go to great lengths to protect the penguins," Mimi commented. "And it's hard to say who's chasing who," she added, looking down at a bundled-up figure below awkwardly chasing the birds off the field. The penguins seemed to have minds of their own. They scampered and slid on their bellies in all directions despite futile attempts to herd them in one direction.

"Three, six, nine, twelve, fifteen...," Grant counted hurriedly by threes to find out how many penguins were on the field before the plane flew too far away. "I think they're emperor penguins," he cried, noting their black and white coloring and large, pudgy bodies. "I want to see them up close! I read they're almost as tall as I am!"

Soon the *Mystery Girl* touched down on the nearby ice floe, crunching and skidding on the smooth ice. It took all of Papa's efforts at the

3

controls to keep the plane from sliding this way and that. As the aircraft sputtered to an unsteady halt, Mimi said, "Does it feel to you like the plane's rocking?"

Papa replied, "Well, we ARE on a big floating ice cube."

Everyone jumped at the loud splitting sound. "What was THAT?" Christina asked.

"I wonder if this ice floe is strong enough to hold the plane," Mimi said as she peeked out the window with one eye open and one eye closed, looking for any cracks in the ice.

"They wouldn't have asked us to land here if it wasn't," Papa concluded. As if to verify Papa's words, another plane landed further down the ice floe. "But I didn't expect to share an ice floe with

another plane," he added. "I guess lots more people are coming here as scientists come up with better ways to deal with the cold."

Everyone sat silently, listening to the mournful cracking and moaning of the huge block of ice below them. Christina imagined the plane slipping off the floe—or falling through the ice into the water! Grant joined his hands together and said a quick prayer that everyone would be safe.

"Good idea, Grant," Christina said. "I sure hope we can get off this thing soon!"

Trying to keep his mind off the crunching ice, Grant picked up a pair of binoculars and counted the penguins again. They were now safely on one side of the landing strip.

"Hey, there's one missing!" Grant said to Christina, a bit concerned. "There were 21 penguins, and now I only count 20."

"Are you positive?" Christina said, taking a count herself. "Maybe you missed one."

"No, I didn't!" Grant retorted. "I am good at counting and math!" Christina knew he was good with numbers. *Something about the possible missing penguin made Christina uneasy but*

she couldn't say what. Little did she know one missing penguin would snowball into one big mystery!

Cold Feet and Hot Cocoa

"We've been in this plane for hours," Grant complained.

"It is late in the day but the sun doesn't seem to be going anywhere fast," Mimi commented.

"It's November, start of the long austral summer with six months of daylight!" Papa remarked.

"Mimi, it looks like the plane won't fall through the ice," Grant asked. "Can we get out?"

"No, we stay inside," Mimi ordered. "It's way too cold out there!"

Papa said, "The ice floe's rocking too much. It could be dangerous." He then opened a window to give the kids a clearer view of the floe. A blast of frigid air slapped Grant in the face, taking his breath away.

"Papa! Close it!" Grant screamed. "It feels like razors scraping my face!"

"*Ohhhhhh*," Mimi said, wrapping her red scarf around her face and short blond hair. "And you want to go out there? Now do you see how cold it is?"

Grant nodded, cupping his fist around his cold, red nose.

At last, a message blared on the plane's radio saying the *Mystery Girl* could now land at the real sea-ice landing. The penguins had been cleared.

As the *Mystery Girl* descended a second time, Grant got a good view of the penguins on the side of the landing strip. There were indeed just twenty. "I know I saw one more, Christina," Grant insisted.

"Maybe it dove into the water at the edge of the ice floe," Christina suggested.

The kids scanned the horizon for the missing penguin and could only see an eerie, desolate landscape with just a shed, two red trucks, and McMurdo Station in the distance. On arrival, the airport attendant, wrapped from head to boots in red, warmly greeted them.

"Welcome to the ice! I'm Al," he stammered, a cloud of steam shooting from his mouth, and specs of ice flying from his mustache. "I guess I don't need to tell you to walk quickly to the shed. You're not dressed for this weather!" He glanced at Papa's cowboy boots. "You'll need some warmer boots here, pardner!"

Papa grinned through his shivers. "Whatever you say!" he said.

The attendant then told Papa that his host, Dr. Orlav, would be here shortly to take them to McMurdo Station. They hustled to the shed to wait. "It's s-s-sooo c-c-c-cold!" Christina stuttered between chattering teeth.

Excited about being in Antarctica, Grant peppered the attendant with questions. "Why is everything red?" he asked. "Your clothes are red, and the trucks outside are red."

"That's so we can easily be seen in case there's a blizzard—when everything's white!" the airport worker replied.

"Mimi will love it here then," Christina said. "She loves red!"

11

"Were you the one who cleared the field of penguins?" Grant asked.

"No, that was the other guy, Brett," he answered.

"What a cool job," Grant said, totally in awe of the man.

"It's not a cool job. It's a COLD job," the attendant complained.

"Did you know that one of the penguins is missing?" Grant asked. "You didn't get them all."

"Why do you say that?" the attendant asked, raising his eyebrow.

"I counted the birds before you cleared the field and then again after you cleared it," Grant replied, as he sniffed his stuffy nose. He was **adamant**, and he stuck out his chin to show confidence. "There's one missing."

"I'm sure Brett got them all," the attendant stated firmly. "You must've seen a mirage," he continued. "Antarctica is so dry it's considered a desert. Like in a desert, people see mirages here. So...maybe you saw a phantom penguin!"

"Okay, Grant," Mimi said as she tousled Grant's blond, curly hair. "I've heard enough

about missing penguins." She touched Grant's forehead. It was a little warm, despite the frigid air. Mimi said to Papa, "Grant's a little cranky, and doesn't look his usual perky self. I think he's coming down with a cold."

The attendant poured some hot coffee for Mimi and Papa. He offered some hot cocoa to Grant. He shook his head and sat with his arms crossed. Christina gladly took a cup of cocoa and leaned back against the shed wall to sip the delicious, steamy brew. She heard a strange, muffled, squealing sound and footfalls. *She turned her ear to the wall. Was she hearing things? Surely that was no mirage!*

3

Another Mirage in the Icy Desert?

An odd-looking vehicle resembling a red box on treads crunched along the ice to the airport. Its driver was Dr. Magnus Orlav, a friend of Papa's and a scientist at McMurdo Station. He had invited Papa and the family to Antarctica so Mimi could do research for her next book. Dr. Orlav expertly parked the vehicle and strode over the ice. It was clear that the tall, burly Russian with the ice-covered, handlebar mustache was used to Antarctica.

"Magnus, it's great to see you!" Papa said, slapping Dr. Orlav on the back. "You remember

my wife, Carole." Mimi stood on her tiptoes to hug the massive man.

Dr. Orlav turned and smiled at the kids. "So, Bob, are these the grandkids you bragged about in your letter?" he asked.

"Yep," Papa said as he put an arm around Christina. "This is my granddaughter, Christina. And this fellow," Papa added, pointing to Grant, who was still in a huff with his arms crossed, "is Grant, my grandson."

"It looks like you've got something on your mind, young man," Dr. Orlav said, twirling the end of his mustache, making snowflakes flutter to the floor.

"I do," Grant muttered, still looking down.

Mimi explained, "Grant's moping today. He counted some penguins as we landed and thinks one is missing. He's upset because he thinks no one's taking him seriously."

"I think you may be right, Grant," Dr. Orlav observed, "because something tells me you're good at counting. It's hard to count penguins," he added. "I do it all the time and I sometimes miscount, so I would know."

"You do?" Grant asked, not believing his ears. Here was someone who understood!

"Let's get aboard the Hagglund," Dr. Orlav said, yanking open the huge side door of the vehicle. "We can talk about penguins later."

The airport attendant and his helper, Brett, came out to help load the baggage. After everyone settled into their seats, Dr. Orlav started the engine and the vehicle jumped to life. Soon, they were crunching along over the ice.

Grant, excited at riding in this "totally awesome" vehicle, soon forgot about the missing penguin. "What is this called again—a Bag Land?"

"No," Dr. Orlav replied with a laugh, "it's a Hagglund, built in Sweden. We use it to transport up to six people."

"Riding on these treads instead of wheels feels funny," Grant said. He looked at Christina and giggled. "My teeth are jiggling!"

"It's a little bumpy," Dr. Orlav agreed. "But it's a safe way for traveling over thin ice and ice floes—like right now. If the Hagglund were to break through ice to the water underneath, it'll still float."

"That's comforting to know," Mimi said. "But how do you get the vehicle back on the ice once you've gone through it?"

Dr. Orlav laughed. "Just another problem—one of many we face constantly at the South Pole. Everyday living can be very difficult at times."

Papa explained, "Dr. Orlav is here at the South Pole to study penguins."

"REALLY?" Grant asked, leaning forward to hear the conversation above the roar of the vehicle. "Is THAT why you said you counted penguins?"

"I actually run a ranch where we study penguins," Dr. Orlav replied. "Instead of cattle, we have penguins!"

"COOOL!" Grant cried, thoroughly impressed. He couldn't imagine a more fun job than running a penguin ranch.

Christina asked, "What are you researching?"

"Many things," Dr. Orlav answered, "such as penguin diving and eating habits, and how they take care of their young. Scientists really don't know that much about the birds."

"It must be an interesting job," Christina commented.

"Having a job down here, even a boring one, is better than having nothing to do," Dr. Orlav said. "There's very little entertainment and few places to go. During the winter, everyone has to stay indoors. Antarctica actually doubles in size in the winter because so much ice forms around the coastline. So, work keeps us out of trouble!"

"Where's your ranch?" Grant asked, leaning even farther forward, nearly touching the front seat.

"It's on the outskirts of Camp McMurdo, not so far away," Dr. Orlav answered.

"Could I visit it?" Grant asked. "I would LOVE to see the penguins! But I know it's forbidden to get close to them."

"Oh, you can see them. Or better yet," Dr. Orlav answered. "How would you like to work at the ranch?"

"NO KIDDING? FOR REAL?" Grant asked, totally amazed.

"For real," Dr. Orlav said. "Like I said, it's best that everybody has something to do. You and

19

Christina can count penguins. It would be great if Mimi helped out with our weekly newspaper and your Papa helped fly supplies to a nearby station."

Everyone looked at each other. "That's a deal!" Mimi and Papa said together.

"When do we begin, Magnus?" Papa asked.

"As soon as I get you settled and rested," Dr. Orlav replied.

Christina gazed out the window. It was going to be so much fun to work with penguins, she thought. She then noticed one of the four-wheel-drive trucks parked at the airport suddenly passing them by. A big red and blue canvas bag lay in the back of the truck. But it was moving—something inside the bag was alive and squirming around!

"Grant, look!" Christina cried. "Something's moving in that bag!"

"My missing penguin?" Grant whispered.

Dr. Orlav parked the Hagglund in front of a dormitory he called Hotel California. He helped his guests unload their luggage. As Grant grabbed his backpack, a piece of paper flew out.

Stay away from
the penguins!
They are <u>off limits!</u>

Grant showed the note to Christina. "Is someone upset I noticed a missing penguin?" he asked, concern in his big blue eyes.

"We'll see," Christina replied.

A Cold
in the Cold

Dr. Orlav took Papa, Mimi, Grant and Christina to their rooms, which were much smaller than a typical hotel room. Grant and Christina shared a room just big enough for bunk beds, a small chest, and a closet. There was hardly room to turn around!

"Settle in and get comfortable," Dr. Orlav said. "I know it's a bit tight, but at least it's warm! This is luxury for the South Pole."

"Oh, it'll do quite well!" Mimi responded. "I was wondering if we'd be sleeping in tents without heat!"

"A few years ago, that would have been the case," Dr. Orlav answered. "Now, we can give

23

visitors the basics of comfort and safety. That's one reason your grandchildren were able to come here."

"I heard there are not many kids here," Grant said, as he sniffled and rubbed his nose.

"You're a rare species," Dr. Orlav replied, laughing. "So don't be surprised if the scientists put you under the microscope, so to speak. They'll definitely notice you!" Dr. Orlav headed down the hall. "Now, come with me and I'll show you where you can use email and the Internet."

"What about cell phones?" Christina asked. "Mine doesn't seem to work here."

"I'm sorry, it won't work here," Dr. Orlav answered. "We use walkie-talkies instead. I'll give each of you one to carry around." He opened his black leather bag and passed them out. Then he showed his guests how to use the walkie-talkies. He added, "Always carry it with you outdoors. You never know when you might need it."

Later that evening, although the sun was still shining, Dr. Orlav took the family to the cafeteria in Building 155. "You're lucky to come when you did," he said, scanning the dinner menu posted on a bulletin board. "Freshies are being served tonight!"

"Freshies?" Christina asked. By the sound of his voice, freshies must be something fabulous, she thought.

"Fresh vegetables! Carrots, peas and broccoli!" Dr. Orlav answered with gusto. "They've just been flown in today. The plane that landed after you must have had them on board!"

"Ugh!" Grant complained, a little disappointed. "Who could get excited about peas and broccoli?"

"The OAE, that's who!" Dr. Orlav answered. "The Old Antarctic Explorers—the guys who've been through a winter down here! They've had to eat canned and dried food for months on end. You know you're an OAE when about mid-winter, you want fresh vegetables more than chocolate!"

"I don't think I'll ever be an OAE!" Grant said, eyeing the vegetables like they were poison.

After picking up their food in a cafeteria-style line, everyone sat down at a long, rectangular table with several scientists and workers at McMurdo Station. Grant watched the local residents dig into the freshies and remarked, "This is like a bunch of vegetarians at a veggie Thanksgiving!" Grant gladly passed his portion of carrots to one man eagerly munching on a carrot stalk. "Take mine," he said, "I haven't touched it."

Mimi said, "Grant, you're coming down with a cold. You need the vitamins in those 'freshies'."

"And the other people here don't want to catch your cold!" Christina blurted out.

A scientist next to Christina wearing a thick knitted scarf warily asked, "Does the boy have a cold?"

"We think he's getting one," Christina replied. "He's sniffling a lot and his mood is off."

The scientist moved a few seats away from the kids. "Sorry," he said, "but those of us who've been here a while don't have resistance to the current 'bugs.' If that boy has a cold, everyone else here will get one, too!"

Two men sat down in the space vacated by the scientist. One was short and pudgy with a full beard and mustache. The other was tall and lean with a close-cropped beard. He wore a Yankees baseball cap. The taller man said, "I see we have the fingys joining us for dinner tonight."

Christina recognized the two men. She asked, "Are you the men who met us at the airport?"

"Yeah, that was us," the shorter man replied. "Hidden behind the snow and ice on our faces. I'm Brett Brackets. I'm a truck driver."

"And I'm Al Pearson," the tall man said. "Besides handling traffic at the air strip, I also work in the vehicle repair shop. I fix just about anything that moves on treads or wheels."

"What's a fingy?" Grant asked.

"A fingy is a newcomer to the Pole," Al replied.

Christina noticed the taller man's baseball cap. "Mr. Pearson, you must like the Yankees," she said.

Grant butted in, "Can you get the Yankees games on TV down here, Mr. Pearson?"

"I see baseball games over the Internet—or watch a video replay later," Mr. Pearson said. "My friend Brett helps with the Internet. He knows a lot about it since he uses the Internet to take care of business."

"What brings you to the South Pole, Mr. Brackets?" Christina asked. Mr. Brackets had a distracted air about him, like his mind was on many things.

"Oh...you can call me Brett," he replied. "I am a writer. I wanted the experience of living in Antarctica. Driving a truck lets me meet a lot of people, and I get to visit the research stations."

A young woman sat down across from Christina. "Hello, I'm Dr. Frieda Ortiz from Argentina," she said.

28

"What do you do?" Christina asked.

"I study meteorites," she said, with a warm smile. "You can call me Dr. Frieda." I like her, Christina thought. She's so friendly! "And why are you and your brother visiting this c-c-cold place?" she asked.

"We were invited by my grandfather's friend, Dr. Orlav," Christina said.

"Oh, the penguin scientist!" Dr. Frieda observed. "This is certainly the place for penguins!"

"That's why I came here!" Grant cried in a loud, nasally voice. He wiped his dripping nose with his napkin. "I love penguins. Dr. Orlav wants Christina and me to count the penguins at his ranch!"

Everyone looked over at Grant. Some faces were frowning.

Al Pearson said, "That boy will be sporting snotsicles before long!"

"Snotsicles?" Grant asked. "Do they taste good? Are they like popsicles?"

The room rocked with laughter.

Al said, "Kid, you have a dripping nose. When you go outside in this weather, the drip

29

will turn to ice—like an icicle, except it's made of snot!"

Grant burst out laughing. He turned to Christina. "I'll give you a snotsicle for a popsicle!"

Christina jumped back and wrinkled her nose. "Gross!" she cried.

"That's enough for me!" said the scientist with the neck scarf. "I don't need to hear that when I'm eating!"

"Pay no attention to him," whispered Dr. Frieda to Grant and Christina. "He's always grouchy, especially during the winter. People around here call him 'Grouchy Pants'."

"Why 'Grouchy Pants'?" Grant asked, giggling at the funny name.

"His last name is Grouchenpanz," Dr. Frieda replied. "He's from Austria."

"From Austria?" Grant said. "Maybe he doesn't like the 'austral summer.' Get it?" he added, elbowing Christina.

"You and your jokes," Christina said. But that was pretty clever, she thought, smiling to herself.

After dinner, Christina and Grant returned to their room to find a little stuffed toy, sitting on the door handle. It was a penguin chick—with a note tied around its neck!

BEWARE!
Kids with colds should stay indoors and play with toys.

Grant asked, "Why would someone write a note like this? It's like the other note!"

"Maybe it's because you sounded like you have a cold and everyone else is afraid of getting it," Christina replied. *Or maybe, she thought, it has*

something to do with your job of counting penguins. This is a ***benevolent*** way of saying, "Don't do it!"

Danger in the Deep Freeze

Exhausted from the day's adventures, Christina and Grant were eager to climb into their bunk beds and snuggle under the fluffy down comforters. "Now I know what this curtain is for," Christina commented, sliding the black curtain across the window to block out the sun, still shining late at night.

The next morning, Grant was feeling much better but his nose dripped like a faucet. He jumped out of bed—he had a plan to see what "snotsicles" looked like!

Christina, still in her top bunk, yawned, and asked, "Grant, what are you doing up so early? It's five o'clock in the morning!"

"I'm going outside to grow some snotsicles," he said, pulling a thick sweater over his blond curls.

"Gross, again!" Christina cried, her long brown hair flying as she tumbled back into her cozy bunk. "Don't come back here with snotsicles if you want to eat breakfast with me!"

Grant added a thick jacket, hat and gloves, and ran outside. The early-morning frigid air made his eyes water and nose run. He charged into the wind, blowing his nose to make more "stuff" run out.

Al Pearson passed Grant on his way to the cafeteria for breakfast. "Growing snotsicles?" he asked, smiling at the two long, fat yellow icicles hanging from each of Grant's nostrils. "Isn't it cool how they grow?"

"Hi, Mr. Pearson!" Grant said. "It's not only COOOL, it's FREEEEEEZING!"

Grant ran in circles, showing off his snotsicles to anyone walking by. Suddenly, his feet flew out from under him.

WHACK!

He crashed into a man in a yellow, fur-lined jacket. It was Dr. Grouchy Pants! The two slid down the sidewalk, arms and legs jumbled together. Grant ended up on top of Dr. Grouchenpanz, his snotsicles dripping on the horrified man's face. "You're disgusting!" he shouted, pushing Grant away.

"Most people try to get rid of their snotsicles," Al Pearson said, as he pulled Grant and Dr. Grouchenpanz to their feet. "You might want to try that," he added.

Grant stared at his reflection in a window to see if the snotsicles survived the fall. They were still there!

"Hey, Mr. Pearson, will you take a picture of me with my camera?" Grant asked. Al smiled and nodded. After approving the digital snapshot, Grant carefully snapped off the snotsicles before going back inside. When Grant returned to his room, Christina and Mimi were sorting clothes.

"Grant, what are you doing outside with that cold?" Mimi asked sharply. "Other people here obviously don't want to get it. I hear they call it the 'Crud'."

"I feel a little better, Mimi," Grant said. "I wanted to go outside."

"You need to rest for a little while," Mimi ordered.

"Look at this, Christina!" Grant said as he showed Christina his camera with the digital image Al just took of him.

Christina burst out laughing. She cried out through giggles, "Mimi, look at this! Grant looks just like a walrus with tusks!"

"Well, growing snotsicles really cleared out my head and nose," Grant observed. "I feel wonderful now!"

"That may be," Mimi replied, glad to hear he felt better. "But for the sake of the rest of us, just lie low for a little while."

Once Grant climbed back into bed, Mimi and Christina brought things they had picked up at the library. Mimi gave him a copy of a famous

book called *Mr. Popper's Penguins* and a DVD recording of the movie, *Happy Feet.*

Christina, Papa and Mimi hadn't quite recovered from their long trip so they decided to take it easy by staying close to the dormitory. The three attended a talk for American newcomers given by the U.S. marshal. It was about observing laws of the United States while visiting the Pole.

The marshal, named Bill Merrick, explained that no government ruled the South Pole. Each visitor abided by the laws of his or her own country. Mr. Merrick said it was his job to enforce the law for the United States. Any American who commits a crime will be punished. Anyone who suspected criminal behavior, or was a crime victim, should contact Mr. Merrick.

Papa said in a joking manner, leaning back in his chair, "Christina, you're always solving crimes. You'd better get his name, just in case!"

A chill slithered down Christina's back. Even though she knew Papa meant to make a joke,

something told her that crimes and danger were coming her way. She just might need Mr. Merrick!

MacTown Downtown

The next day, Grant felt good enough to join Mimi, Papa, and Christina on a tour of McMurdo Station, or "MacTown," as the residents called it. Dr. Orlav wanted to show his guests some of the 100 buildings that made up the station.

Everyone gathered by the door for the tour. Dr. Orlav, who was bundled head to toe in Antarctic wear, said, "Before we leave the building, let me inspect your ECW. It's 15 degrees outside!"

"That's not my underwear, is it?" Grant asked. "I did put on a clean pair—and even a pair of long underwear!"

Dr. Orlav laughed. "No, ECW is not your underwear," he replied. "But I'm glad you put on

clean pair! ECW is short for Extreme Cold Weather gear. You should have gotten a whole bunch of it when you arrived. We issue down parkas, layers of polar fleece pants and shirts, snow pants, snow goggles, wool socks, and thermal boots we call Bunny Boots!"

"I have my Bunny Boots on!" Christina cried. "I love that name," she whispered to Mimi.

Mimi asked, "Isn't 15 degrees rather warm for the South Pole?"

Dr. Orlav wrapped Christina's knit scarf twice around her neck. "When we say a certain temperature here," he explained, "we always mean 'minus.' It just goes without saying here that the temperature is below zero!"

"So you're saying it is -15 degrees?" Mimi concluded.

"Yes, ma'am," he replied. "No need to say minus when it's almost never plus!"

"It looks like you're dressed to my standards!" Dr. Orlav observed, looking over his guests. "Remember, never expose your skin, and not just to the cold and wind. Even though it is deadly cold outside, the sun is still fearsome when it's shining," he added. "Do you know why?"

"The ozone!" Christina piped up. "I read that there is a thinning of the ozone layer above Antarctica and that lets in the super-strong rays of the sun."

"That's right," Dr. Orlav answered, rubbing some sunscreen on Grant's nose.

The group boarded the shuttle bus, and started their tour around MacTown. They got a good look at the black volcanic rocks that form the foundation of McMurdo Station.

Dr. Orlav explained that MacTown is located at the southernmost point of solid ground that ships can reach. The community has a hospital, fire department, and video store. Dr. Orlav also showed them the Chalet, the "headquarters" where important officials running American Antarctic operations worked.

"What are all those flags flying for?" Grant asked, as they passed a long row of vivid flags fluttering in the breeze.

"Each flag represents a country doing research in Antarctica," Dr. Orlav answered, twirling the end of his mustache. "The countries of the world have decided that Antarctica should

not belong to anybody or any one nation. It should be an international refuge for peaceful scientific study."

"Is that why we keep hearing that the wildlife, plant life, and minerals are protected, and nobody can take them out of here?" Christina asked.

"Yes," Dr. Orlav replied. "Those things are not to be exploited, taken, or used for private purposes."

"So what are the scientists studying here?" Grant asked. "It's just snow and ice!"

"Oh, there's lots to study here," Dr. Orlav replied. "For example, geologists study plate tectonics and meteorites, biologists study how organisms adapt to harsh temperatures, and other scientists are studying the hole in the ozone layer above Antarctica. Astronomers have a clearer view of space here than anywhere else on Earth!"

"Well," Grant said, winking at Christina, "this place is pretty cool, if you get my drift!" Christina giggled.

Dr. Orlav urged his guests take a short walk around "downtown." As Christina and Grant hobbled through the snow and ice, careful not

to fall, Christina wondered if the missing penguin was taken for non-research purposes. Just then, a huge red bus marked "Ivan the Terra" caught her eye as it shuddered by, carrying workers to an outstation.

"Grant!" Christina yelled, pointing at the bus, "Look what's written on the side!"

Hey FINGYS! PENGUINS aRe NOT TOYS— STay away FROM THeM! aNTaRCTICa RULeS!

That message sure sounded familiar!

Fishy Business

The next stop on Dr. Orlav's tour was the Crary Science and Engineering Center. While Papa, Dr. Orlav, and Grant explored the laboratory, Mimi and Christina decided to listen to Dr. Frieda's talk on meteorites.

Dr. Ortiz explained that scientific teams have found more than 20,000 meteorites in Antarctica. "Antarctica is the best place to find meteorites. Can anyone tell me why?" she asked the audience.

Brett Brackets, the truck driver who called himself a writer, raised his hand. "The snow and ice make meteorites easy to find—black on white!" he said. "And there are no rocks and dirt to hide them from view."

"Good answer!" Dr. Ortiz replied. "Here are some pictures of meteorites we found just lying on the ice." She flipped on a switch and a huge

image appeared on the screen. "See how clearly the black rocks appear on the ice?" she asked. "Even the little ones are easy to spot." She went on to say why meteorites are important. "Meteorites come from the asteroid belt between Mars and Jupiter, other planets, and even the moon. They tell us much about the universe beyond our little Earth. Each new one may have something more to tell us."

Mimi raised her hand with a question. "I understand some meteorites are very valuable because they contain precious metals," she said. "I guess they could be used for fine jewelry, couldn't they?"

"Oh, yes," Dr. Frieda replied. "Some contain gold, titanium, and other precious metals. By the way, while we are on the subject of valuable metals, all of you must know something. Nothing found here in Antarctica can be claimed as yours and taken home. These natural objects include penguins and whales. They are protected, and can only be handled for scientific purposes."

After the talk, Christina and Mimi joined Dr. Orlav, Papa, and Grant.

"How about a visit to the aquarium?" Dr. Orlav suggested. "You won't find one like it in the states!"

"Why is it so special?" Grant asked.

"The tanks only have local Antarctic marine life," Dr. Orlav answered. "They contain sea animals recently retrieved from the ocean for study purposes."

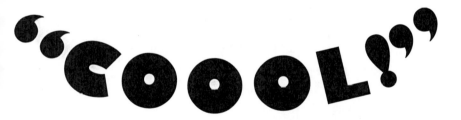

"COOL!"

Grant said, amazed at all the neat jobs people did at the Pole.

They visited a tank full of fish with "antifreeze" in their blood to keep from freezing. They also saw starfish, sea spiders and Antarctic cod.

"Any questions?" Dr. Orlav asked.

"I forgot what kind of fish penguins eat," Grant said. "You must know."

"Each species has its favorite food," Dr. Orlav explained. "Our emperor penguins here like to eat krill. It's a tiny fish that travels in huge schools. Penguins have to eat a lot of krill to fill up."

Trying to keep a serious face, Grant asked, "What's their favorite salad?"

"Huh?" Dr. Orlav asked, twirling his mustache. "Well, I'm afraid I don't know."

"Iceberg lettuce!" Grant replied, with a roar of laughter. "And they like to drink out of beakers! Get it, beak-ers?"

Everyone laughed at Grant's silly jokes. Even Christina had to admit he had come up with some good ones lately. Dr. Orlav then let the kids explore the aquarium while he, Papa, and Mimi enjoyed a cup of coffee.

Grant and Christina crept between the gurgling fish tanks. They peered at the strange creatures swimming among rising bubbles and dark, gloomy rocks.

"What's that sound?" Christina whispered to Grant as they approached the end of the darkened room.

"It's coming from behind that door," Grant whispered back. He peeked into the crack of the open door.

"It's a seal!" Grant exclaimed, opening the door for Christina to see a slick, shiny gray seal flopping around in a huge tank. It poked its head over the top of the tank and made loud barking sounds.

"Who's there?" a booming voice sounded from behind the kids.

Christina and Grant gasped and bumped into each other in fear.

"Oh, it's you, Brett!" Christina cried, letting out a sigh. "You scared us!"

"Seeing Antarctica's wildlife up close, are you?" Brett asked. His facial expression and voice were not friendly.

The kids nodded, feeling slightly scared and guilty for sneaking into the room with the seal.

Brett was carrying a large plastic bag marked "Live Krill." He said, "That's a baby Weddell seal. Weddell seals live further south than any other mammal. It lost its mother so we're raising it here. You kids need to move along now," he added, motioning to the door.

The kids met up with Mimi, Papa, and Dr. Orlav. As they were leaving the aquarium, a lab worker approached Dr. Orlav. He asked if his ranch had received an extra shipment of krill. When Dr. Orlav said no, the lab worker reported that krill had gone missing at the lab.

Dr. Orlav looked concerned as he twirled the tip of his mustache. After the lab worker left, Papa asked Dr. Orlav why he was worried.

"This is the second time somebody has lost krill," Dr. Orlav explained. "We lost some last month. Now the lab is missing some. I'd sure like to know what is going on!"

Christina's mind began to race. *Was the missing krill connected to the missing penguin? And why was Brett carrying a bag of krill?*

8

Ride 'Em, Cowboy!

The next day, Dr. Orlav arrived at Hotel California to take Christina and Grant to the penguin ranch. "I have a treat for you today, my children," he said as he helped them clamber up into the Hagglund.

"What is it? What is it?" Grant asked, his blue eyes wide with anticipation.

"You'll see!" Dr. Orlav replied with a smile.

Dr. Orlav brought them to a garage with two shiny red vehicles parked out front.

"Aren't those snowmobiles?" asked Christina. "Cooooooool!!!" gasped Grant.

"Sort of," Dr. Orlav replied. "Actually, they're our own special Antarctic version called 'skidoos.' Hop on board and Al will show you how to ride them!"

Once Grant got the hang of skidoo riding, he wheeled around in a big circle, whooping, "Ride 'em, cowboy!" Then the group sped out to the penguin ranch on their "horses," with Dr. Orlav in the lead.

Christina loved the skidoo ride but could not believe how much colder it felt with the wind blowing in her face. "Aren't you cold, Grant?" she asked, glancing behind her. But Grant was not there! "Grant? Grant, where are you?" she cried. "Dr. Orlav, we have to find Grant!"

Dr. Orlav circled back around to Christina. "Let's retrace our steps and see where he went," Dr. Orlav suggested. "Don't worry; he can't have gone far."

"WHOOO HOOO!!"

Grant screeched with excitement as he careened down an icy hill. "Hey, where is

everybody?" he asked, realizing that he had become separated from the others when he decided to take a trip down that inviting little hill. He looked left. He looked right. Everything was white! He was lost! He reached for his cell phone in his pocket. Oh, no, it won't work, he remembered. His hand brushed something else in his pocket. It was the walkie-talkie!

"Dr. Orlav, it's Grant!" he yelled into the receiver. "Help! I'm lost!"

Just then, Christina and Dr. Orlav appeared over the horizon. "There you are!" Christina yelled. "Don't ever disappear like that again!" Dr. Orlav decided that both kids would ride right next to him the rest of the way to the ranch.

Dr. Orlav proudly showed the kids around the ranch, which consisted of a corral surrounded by

a few large sheds for work and storage. Inside the corral, four or five emperor penguins waddled around. A couple of other penguins dove in and out of the water through deep holes dug into the ice.

Dr. Orlav explained that everyone needed to help with the common chores like cleaning up after the birds. "I will **allocate** some work between the two of you," he added. "Grant, your job will be to count the adult penguins at the beginning and at the end of the day. Also, you need to keep track of which penguins go in the water and for how long. We want to make sure we don't lose any. Get to know them and recognize them by their looks."

"Awesome!" Grant cried, pumping his fist in the air.

"When you count one, be sure to mark its head with this red water-soluble paint," Dr. Orlav explained, pointing to several cans of red paint. "You don't want to count the same bird twice!"

"Do they have names?" Grant asked.

"A few of the standouts do," Dr. Orlav answered, "like that big bird with the white star

on its wing. We call him 'The General' because he not only wears his rank on his sleeve, but he acts like a general. He's the top bird at the ranch."

"And me? What do I do, Dr. Orlav?" Christina asked, already prepared to take notes with a pen and paper.

"I want you to count the chicks in the morning and evening," Dr. Orlav directed. "It's hatching season. New chicks make their appearance every day. Keep tabs on them—you can even name them—and most importantly, make sure they don't get into trouble!"

"How do they get into trouble?" Christina asked.

"Any number of ways," Dr. Orlav said, "like poking their noses into paint cans, diving in the water after their parents, or getting stepped on. Like kittens and puppies, they always seem to find their share of trouble!"

The kids were thrilled to get close to the penguins. As Grant made his morning count, he daubed their heads with the paint. "Hey, Christina," he yelled, while passing a wet brush over the head of a bird, "they're not afraid of humans!"

"Grant," Christina called back, "watch out!"

Too late! Grant felt a sharp pinch on his bottom. He swung around, finding a penguin hanging on to his seat pocket by its pointy beak. The bird swung around with him, not even close to letting go!

"Christina! Help!" Grant yelped. "I can't get rid of him!"

"What do you have in your pocket?" Christina asked, running over to help her brother.

"A piece of fish from there!" Grant shouted, pointing to a barrel sitting next to a nearby shed.

Christina dashed to the barrel and yanked out a piece of half-frozen fish. She hung it front of the bird's nose. It worked! The bird let go of Grant and grabbed the fish.

Grant jumped away and both kids watched with relief as the The General waddled off to munch on his treat. "Boy!" Grant exclaimed, panting. "I guess he is 'King of the Ranch'!"

Later that afternoon, Christina sat next to the penguin corral to rest her legs. "Wait, what's going on?" she cried, as two little chicks wriggled under the corral fence and began to waddle away!

"You're not getting away from me!" she shouted, charging after the furry little fellows racing for the open door of a shed.

Just then, a freckled-face ranch worker named Fred stepped out of the shed, carrying an oil can. The chicks ran under Fred's feet.

Fred's feet shot out from under him and he tumbled to the ice, spilling oil all over the baby penguins. "Oh, no!" Christina wailed, feeling horrible that she couldn't prevent the chicks from getting soaked in the dark, gooey oil.

Fred wrapped one of the birds in a dry cloth, and yelled, "Quick, we can't waste time. Grab the other one with that rag over there. The chicks are losing body heat!"

Christina wrapped the struggling, slippery chick in the rag and followed Fred into the heated hut. He yelled to Christina, "Take that big bucket

and draw some warm water from that canister. Then bring it here."

Fred thrust the birds in the bucket of water. He grabbed a bottle of dishwashing liquid and splashed a little in the water. Then he began scrubbing the feathers of one of the chicks. "Watch me, and do the same for your bird," he told Christina. The chicks resisted every step of the way, feathers flying everywhere. After several rinses, Fred said, "Well, Shiny and Baldy, you're clean, but you'll have to stay in this shed until your feathers grow out!"

"Can I knit sweaters for Shiny and Baldy?" Christina asked Fred. "I don't want them to freeze!"

"Yeah, that'd be a great idea!" Fred answered. "The chicks need insulation from the cold! I can only keep them so long in a cramped cage."

That evening, Christina and Grant told their grandparents about their day. Grant rubbed his backside and said, "It was fun but it was hard work! My bottom's still a little sore, too."

"I need to start knitting sweaters for Shiny and Baldy," Christina added, pulling a ball of yarn and knitting needles from her suitcase.

"I'll help," Mimi offered. "That way the birds can get their sweaters faster! We can have them ready when you go back to your new jobs."

9

Antarctica Makes Heroes the Hard Way

The next day was not a workday so Christina and Grant went sightseeing in the area around McMurdo Station. Dr. Orlav packed the kids into the Hagglund. The first stop on the tour was the Pegasus Ice Runway.

"Pegasus is the farthest south of McMurdo's three frozen airstrips," Dr. Orlav explained. "We still use it for the big wheeled aircraft that can't land on snow. We might see a plane or two arriving!"

"Why is the landing field called Pegasus?" Grant asked.

"A plane named Pegasus crashed at the ice strip during bad weather years ago," Dr. Orlav replied. "No one was hurt in the crash but the plane has never been removed."

At the airstrip, everyone explored the old propeller-driven Super Constellation christened "Pegasus." Like a big injured bird, it rested on its side in the ice.

Dr. Orlav told the kids, "That plane reminds us how easily things can go wrong when the weather's bad!"

They stayed at the airport to watch a huge C-17 Globemaster being unloaded. It brought supplies and research equipment from the United States.

After warming up and eating a hot lunch at McMurdo Station, Dr. Orlav took his guests in the opposite direction out of town. While driving in the Hagglund, they could see smoke rising from the distant volcano called Mt. Erebus. Dr. Orlav said it was one of the largest volcanoes in the world.

"Is it a live volcano?" Christina asked.

Dr. Orlav answered, "It erupted recently in the 1980s when volcanic debris as big as cars rained down near the mountain. A research team had to evacuate the area. There is intense volcanic activity in Antarctica. There's always a good chance that this volcano, or others on the continent, could have some kind of eruption."

The Hagglund pulled up to Scott's Discovery Hut. "Here's a good place," Dr. Orlav noted, "to see firsthand the difficulties of the early explorers." He led them into an old, weathered hut surrounded by a porch on three sides.

"This hut was built in 1902," he explained, "by the men of Robert Scott's *Discovery* Expedition in their attempt to get to the South Pole. Since then, it is mainly used to store things since it is hard to heat."

The kids looked around the stark, frozen hut. Ancient supplies of food and provisions were still on shelves in old boxes.

"There's something pretty old out there, too," Dr. Orlav remarked. He pointed to the porch on the south side of the hut. "You might want to check out the mummified seal."

Grant and Christina raced out to the porch. Christina stopped in her tracks. "Ohhhh," she gasped.

Grant yelled as he stared at the cold, hard, black seal remains. "How did it get there?"

"Some of Scott's men just left the carcass there about a hundred years ago," Dr. Orlav explained. "Apparently, they were going to use it for its oil." He winked at the kids. "As you can see, the cold air preserves things pretty well!"

Christina covered her eyes, and then looked the other way, hoping not to throw up!

Back in the hut, Christina asked Dr. Orlav, "Did Robert Scott ever make it to the South Pole?"

"Not during the *Discovery* Expedition," Dr. Orlav replied. "That trip proved too difficult for the sled dogs, so the team couldn't move forward. He reached the Pole on a second expedition in 1912. But, a Norwegian named Roald Amundsen had arrived just 35 days ahead of him. The biggest tragedy was that he and his four team members died on the way back—from slow starvation and bitter cold."

Christina said, "I remember seeing a movie on TV about Shackleton's *Endurance* Expedition. That team had to cross mountains and glaciers, doing incredible things to rescue some of their team members."

"That very same Shackelton used this hut during his *Nimrod* Expedition in 1908, Dr. Orlav noted. "And Scott used it again during that 1912 *Terra Nova* Expedition."

Christina and Grant were amazed by the danger, risks, and isolation that these early explorers encountered. There was danger at every turn! *They had no idea they would face their own share of danger soon enough!*

The Mystery in Icy Antarctica

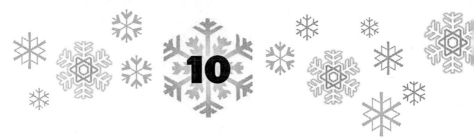

Back at the Ranch

The next day, Grant counted his penguins once again. "17, 18, 19." Grant scratched his head. "I know I had twenty yesterday," he said. "Why do I have one less penguin than I had yesterday?" He ran over to Christina and asked her to help him count them again. They came up with the same count—nineteen!

Alarmed, Christina counted her chicks. She found that one more had hatched, so now she had five chicks. Fred said the new one cracked his shell yesterday and was running about in no time. Christina and Fred hurried to the shed to find Shiny and Baldy looking lonely and naked. They also missed their mamas!

PEEP! PEEP!!

"I put them in a cage warmed by a light bulb," Fred said, "but they just huddle together, making those sad peeps."

"Their sweaters are ready, Fred!" Christina said, pulling two fluffy sweaters from her backpack. "Let's see how they do in this ECW wear! I knitted the red one and my grandmother made the yellow one."

Fred lifted Baldy out of the cage and dressed him in the yellow sweater. Christina carefully slipped the red sweater on Shiny. Then they put the two birds on the floor of the shed. The two chicks looked a little surprised as they waddled,

trying out their new clothes. Suddenly, the two scampered out the door, peeping madly as they headed right toward their mamas.

"Great job, Christina!" Fred said, laughing as he watched the dressed-up chicks rub noses with the mother birds. "It looks like they're quite comfortable!"

Christina grabbed her camera. "Let's take a picture of Shiny and Baldy with their mommies!" she exclaimed. "Sooooo cute!"

The evening penguin count was the same as the morning's, both for Christina and Grant. Grant's missing penguin had not shown up during the day. Grant was still worried. He sent an email to Dr. Orlav to report the missing penguin.

The next day, Christina was pleased to see all her chicks doing well, including the two who were still wearing their sweaters. They made it through the Antarctic "night!"

Grant was not so lucky. He counted his penguins again—now he only had eighteen! This time the missing penguin was that brute, The General, who had tweaked his bottom!

Was Grant seeing things—or not seeing things? What was happening to the penguins?

11

A Bird in the Bag is Worth Two on the Ice

Later that day, on the return trip to McMurdo Station, Dr. Orlav brought the kids along with him to Williams Field. They went to pick up Papa who had flown to an outstation that day. Mimi was warm and toasty back at MacTown working on the newspaper.

Dr. Orlav decided to take a shortcut over a little-used trail.

"Dr. Orlav!" Grant yelled as he jabbed his finger at the front window, "Those black dots over there—are they penguins?"

"Well, I'll be a penguin's uncle!" Dr. Orlav answered. "It looks like emperor penguins have

formed a small rookery! I don't remember seeing another rookery around this area. I guess this will be another place we'll have to stay away from for a while. No exploring here!"

"I know, Dr. Orlav," Grant said. "Natural penguin rookeries are off limits to everybody. But can we take some pictures from here? My camera has a zoom lens."

"Sure," Dr. Orlav said. He parked the Hagglund and the kids jumped out.

As Grant snapped his pictures, Christina explored the area. She spied something blue and red lying behind a clump of ice. Curious, she tiptoed over to it. It was a large canvas bag like the kind she had seen in the back of the truck—the one with something squirming around inside it! She showed Dr. Orlav her find. "Can I take this bag back to McMurdo?" Christina asked Dr. Orlav. "Maybe I can find its owner!"

"Yes, take it, since someone is probably missing it," he answered. "Although I have to say it's a bag commonly used on expeditions here in Antarctica. Do you see a name or ID tag on it?"

"No," Christina answered, inspecting the bag. "It sure smells bad, though!"

"You might have a hard time tracking down the owner," Dr. Orlav remarked. He glanced at his watch. "Oh, we'd better hurry along. We don't want your grandfather waiting in the cold!"

That evening, Christina took a closer look at the red and blue bag. She found a hidden pocket—with a wrinkled piece of paper inside!

"Look at this, Grant!" Christina said, as she handed him the note. "What do you think this means?"

77.801 S
166.703 E
R-chondrite group??

"How should I know?" Grant replied. "Maybe we can look up the words and numbers on the Internet when we get a chance." Christina nodded her head and stuffed the note in her pocket. *Was this a clue to the missing penguins?*

Back at the ranch the next day, Grant was short one more penguin—now there were only 17 adult penguins at the ranch! That was three down from the original 20 birds.

"We better report this," Christina said. "This is serious!" She ran to tell Dr. Orlav, but she had an idea, too.

"Dr. Orlav, do you suppose we could go to that new penguin rookery we saw yesterday?" she asked.

"Why?" Dr. Orlav answered. "I would need permission to go there."

"Well," she answered, "that rookery is near here. Do you think our penguins might have gone there to join a larger group?"

Grant suddenly remembered a joke. "Hey," he interrupted, "why did the penguins cross the road and go somewhere else?"

"I don't know," Dr. Orlav said.

"To go with the floe!" Grant replied, giggling. "I got you!"

Dr. Orlav laughed. "I thought you were asking a serious question, but I should have known better!" he said. "But seriously," he added, "the birds have everything they need here. I don't know if they'd want to go to another rookery. But it's certainly worth a try. I'm just as anxious as you are to find out what's happening to the disappearing penguins!"

Christina asked, "Oh, by the way, Dr. Orlav, has anybody here seen the krill shipment that was meant to go the Crary Lab? Or the one you were missing?"

"No, I just asked the other day," Dr. Orlav answered, twisting the tip of his mustache. "Things HAVE been going missing around here lately, haven't they?"

Christina wondered if the red and blue canvas bag she found—and the note in it—was the key to the mystery. She just had to find the answer!

The Tuxedo Expedition

That evening, the kids forgot about getting on the Internet. They, along with Mimi and Papa, were invited to a party! Dr. Orlav won a huge grant to continue his penguin research and he wanted to celebrate! He asked all the men to come in tuxedos if they had one—in honor of the penguins, of course!

"Oh, Mimi, you look beautiful!" Christina exclaimed, as Mimi appeared in a red silk dress covered with ruffles.

"Thank you so much," Mimi replied, brushing a tiny piece of lint from Papa's black tuxedo.

"Papa, you look just like a penguin!" Grant exclaimed.

"Just trying to fit in down here at the South Pole!" Papa replied, as he straightened his bow tie in the mirror.

Christina couldn't resist a chance to tease her brother. "Grant, you look just like Shiny in your new red sweater!"

Grant shot back, "And you look like a seal in that long, gray, shiny thing!"

"I'll take that as a compliment, my dear brother," Christina replied, tossing back her brown hair, curled in ringlets for the occasion. "Seals are slick!"

At the party, the South Pole scientists and workers were all smiles as they dug into steaks and freshies just flown in from New Zealand. After dinner, Mimi noticed Al Pearson setting up a karaoke system. She nudged Christina. "Wait 'til Grant sees that!" she whispered. "This party will be rocking!"

Grant spied the microphone the minute Al finished setting it up. He scrambled up to the stage.

"Al, can I talk on it, and maybe sing?" Grant asked.

"It's all yours!" Al answered.

Grant cleared his throat and held the microphone to his mouth. "My name is Grant," he said. "We're just visiting here, but you've made us all feel right at home. We didn't get the 'cold shoulder,' if you know what I mean!"

A wave of laughter rippled through the room. Grant was encouraged. "So," he said, "I'd like to sing, *Baby, It's Cold Outside*!"

"You go, Grant!" Christina cried, standing on top of her chair to see the show. Papa grabbed Mimi and headed for the dance floor. Everyone enthusiastically clapped in time as Grant belted out one of his favorite winter melodies.

The party was suddenly cut short when Fred burst through the door.

"Dr. Orlav, two more penguins have gotten out!" Fred exclaimed between huffs and puffs. "I just found them waddling up the street like they were invited to this party!"

"Where are they now?" Dr. Orlav asked.

"I stuffed the birds in the Hagglund," Fred answered, pointing at the front door. "It's parked in the parking lot."

The crowd followed Fred outside. As he opened the door of the Hagglund, two scared birds bolted out, knocking him over in a desperate attempt to escape the vehicle. The birds slid across the ice and looked around. Suddenly, they tobogganed over to Papa and two other men wearing tuxedos. The penguins stood up and rubbed their noses against Papa's waist!

Dr. Orlav laughed. "Bob, they think you're one of them!"

When Papa turned to head back into the Southern Exposure Club, the birds trotted after him. Grant said, "Look! They're all dressed up for the party! Maybe they thought they were invited!"

Dr. Orlav stopped the birds at the door. "Fred, please take these guys back to the ranch before they make a mess of this place!" Fred and Al herded the penguins back into the Hagglund.

While everyone laughed over the incident, Christina wondered how the penguins got out in the first place. *They definitely belonged to Dr. Orlav's ranch. She could tell by daubs of red paint on their heads!*

The next day's weather was stormy, not exactly "a dingle day," as the local British scientists would say. However, it would be the only free day Dr. Orlav could spare. Dr. Orlav checked with the local "weather guesser," an Antarctic term for meteorologist. He decided that

the morning weather would be okay to take Grant, Christina, and Papa on an outing. As Christina suggested, he wanted to see if his penguins were at the new rookery.

Dr. Orlav asked Grant to name this expedition. "We should call it the Tuxedo Expedition," Grant decided, "because it's all about penguins! The birds look like a bunch of guys in tuxedos!"

Before leaving the dorm, Dr. Orlav made doubly sure his guests were wearing ECW gear, just to be on the safe side. He also made sure the Hagglund was well stocked with supplies and fuel. After an hour out, they reached the rookery. Dr. Orlav climbed out of the Hagglund and did a quick count of the penguins he saw clustered in the rookery. "Twenty-nine," Dr. Orlav declared.

"That's what I count, too," Grant agreed, now confident he was not counting phantom penguins!

The curious birds waddled up to Dr. Orlav and his guests. "Inspect the birds for any special features you might recognize—or by any paint marks," he asked Grant and Christina.

"Dr. Orlav!" Grant yelled, as he pointed to two birds. "Those penguins have red paint on the

back of their heads. And that big fellow over there is The General! I couldn't forget him. He's the one that tweaked my bottom!"

"My missing penguins!" Dr. Orlav shouted joyfully, as if he found some lost children.

"I brought my camera," Christina said, yanking it from her coat pocket. "I'm going to take some pictures for evidence!" She walked a complete circle around the birds, snapping pictures from all angles.

Dr. Orlav stood with his hands on his hips and a scowl on his face. "This is something I am going to have to report to my boss!" he exclaimed. "How DID my penguins get here?"

Did the penguins come here themselves, or did somebody bring them here? Did the missing penguin from the airport end up here, too? So many questions! Christina then thought of the red and blue bag found near this rookery. She told herself she would have to get on the Internet that very evening to research those numbers and words she found in the bag.

The Mystery in Icy Antarctica

13

Trapped in the Ice

The weather suddenly turned worse, earlier than expected. The winds kicked up, creating clouds of blowing snow. "Let's get back to the Hagglund before we can't see a foot in front of us," Dr. Orlav warned.

They trudged just a few yards through the stinging snow. The wind was incredibly cold as it made biting entries into Christina's clothing. No one could stay out in this weather for long! Papa's face could hardly be seen behind the beard he had started to grow in the Antarctic. It was covered with icy snow!

Dr. Orlav's mustache was frozen stiff with icicles hanging from the tips. The scientist yelled above the wind, "Be sure to de-gomble before we get in the Hagglund!"

"De-gomble?" Christina, Grant, and Papa answered in one bewildered voice.

"Oh, I forgot you don't know all the jargon yet," Dr. Orlav answered. "Shake off all the snow on your clothes, especially in the nooks and crannies. It'll melt and make a mess in the vehicle." Dr. Orlav pointed at Papa. "Your beard, too," he added.

Snow and ice went flying as the four shook like dogs after a bath. Then everyone jumped into the welcoming heat of the Hagglund. Dr. Orlav had left the motor running to keep the interior toasty.

As Dr. Orlav put the vehicle in gear, Christina detected something red moving in the distance. By the snow it was kicking up, Christina thought the vehicle had to be large, like a truck. She pointed in the direction of the vehicle and said, "Let's follow that!"

Seeing that the vehicle was heading toward MacTown, Dr. Orlav decided to follow it. It kept moving faster and faster, as if it was trying to get away. Suddenly, it veered off the trail. Dr. Orlav tried to keep pace, not wanting to lose sight of it.

THUUUD!

Suddenly, the Hagglund pitched forward and fell...and fell...and fell! It slammed into solid ice, its rear sticking up in the air and its front buried in white. The windshield cracked, but nothing but white could be seen through it. The treads spun madly in the air, going nowhere, except maybe driving the Hagglund deeper into the ice.

"Is everyone all right?" Dr. Orlav asked, twisting in his seat to look for the children in the back. "We're okay," Christina and Grant said, a bit dazed from the experience.

"Me, too," Papa added. "Where are we?"

"In some type of crevasse," Dr. Orlav guessed. "Everybody stay buckled in while I try to move this thing backwards."

The Hagglund wouldn't budge an inch. Dr. Orlav quickly put the gear in neutral to keep the engine running and the interior warm.

The ever-strengthening winds made the wind chill factor far too cold to leave the Hagglund now. Grant looked out the window—he saw total white-out! "Papa, it's like being inside a ping pong ball," Grant remarked. "You just can't see a thing!"

Christina wondered how Grant knew what the inside of a ping pong ball looked like. One thing she knew for certain—they were trapped in ice with a wild Antarctic windstorm raging outside!

14

SOS
Antarctic Style

Dr. Orlav grabbed the portable radio inside the Hagglund. "Sure glad I can contact the outside world with this thing. In this weather, I doubt the walkie-talkies would work! We're just a little too far from MacTown."

Dr. Orlav reached workers at McMurdo Station and explained their situation. He passed on their GPS coordinates so rescuers could find them.

The voice at McMurdo crackled over the radio, "We'll get someone out there just as soon as the wind dies down. Anybody hurt?"

"No," Dr. Orlav replied. "We're fine. Just shaken up. We have two brave kids with us."

"How are you on gas and supplies?" the voice crackled through the intercom.

"I just fueled up before we left so we should be good for hours," Dr. Orlav replied. "We have plenty of food and warm beverages, even for two hungry kids."

Papa signaled to Dr. Orlav he wanted to use the radio. He asked the station to contact Mimi and let her know they were okay.

Now all they could do was hunker down and wait. Dr. Orlav reminded them not to fidget too much so that the Hagglund didn't slip further down into the ice. Christina was amazed that Grant sat so quietly. He wasn't even sick or asleep! She said, "You are as still as a mannequin!"

Grant replied, "I'm just scared stiff!"

It was scary indeed. They were surrounded by a blank whiteness, hearing only the constant crunching and groaning sounds of the ice and the loud

WOOOOOOO

WOOOOOO

WOOOOOO

WOOOOOO

of the wind pelting the top of the Hagglund. Plus, every now and then, they could feel the Hagglund slip downward, bit by bit.

Everyone jumped when the voice over the telecom crackled again. "I have a Carole Marsh here who wants to know how you're doing."

"Mimi!" Grant yelled into the radio receiver. "We're just like the early explorers, trapped in a white-out!"

"Are you okay, Grant?" Mimi asked, anxiety in her voice.

"Yes, ma'am, but it's REEEALLLY scary," replied Grant as Papa took over the radio. Papa explained the details of the accident to her. Then it was Christina's turn to use the radio. She told Mimi about finding Dr. Orlav's missing penguins in the remote rookery they just visited.

After Mimi's call, they tried to lighten up their situation by eating turkey sandwiches and sipping hot cocoa and coffee. At last, the winds died down and the skies cleared. Another crackling message over the radio informed Dr. Orlav that a vehicle was nearby looking for them. Soon they heard distant crunching and the honk of a horn. Dr. Orlav honked his horn in response.

96

Suddenly, the layer of snow disappeared from the window and the ice-covered face of Brett Brackets peered at them. Dr. Orlav opened the window and greeted the driver, "Hi, Brett! We're sure glad to see you!"

"I was headed this way anyway in the Spryte when I heard about your problem over the radio," Brett said, "so I offered to help. I picked up Al Pearson in case you need some repairs."

"Good man," Dr. Orlav said, as he looked over at the Spryte, a big truck on treads. "THAT should be able to pull us out!"

Brett and Al dug around the Hagglund to measure the depth of the hole trapping the vehicle. "It looks like you are in luck," Brett remarked. "This is just a big dip in the ice—more like a shallow ravine than a crevasse. The Hagglund won't slide any further." Everyone let out a huge sigh of relief!

Al said, "I'll attach a cable and we can tow the Hagglund out."

Late in the evening, the group arrived back at the dorm to find a big crowd waiting to greet them

with blankets and hot soup. Christina and Grant pulled off their heavy down parkas. Something fluttered to the floor. It was a newspaper article!

SCIENCE TIMES
Your Source for Science!   Volume 48

VALUABLE GEMSTONES FOUND IN METEORITES!

Christina and Grant looked at each other. "Where did that come from?" Grant said. Christina frowned. *This storm had produced another storm of questions. Who drove away from*

the rookery? And what about the two birds found wandering around near the Southern Exposure Club? How did they get there? And how did this newspaper article get in the Hagglund?

15

A Storm of Questions

At the ranch the next day, Christina had a chance to talk to Dr. Orlav.

"Dr. Orlav," Christina inquired, as she swept up some bird droppings, "how did the two birds get downtown when you had the party?"

"I don't know," Dr. Orlav said. "I can see them going to the new rookery, but not into the town."

Grant tried to make a joke, "We do know why! They wanted to attend your party, of course. They were dressed up for it!"

"Oh, Grant," Christina said. "Get serious." Christina rubbed her forehead and said, "Maybe they were BROUGHT into town!"

"What do you mean?" Dr. Orlav asked.

"Maybe they were being taken somewhere on purpose, some place like the rookery. On the way, while passing near town, the birds managed to escape! Fred just happened to find them near the Southern Exposure Club."

"Penguins being taken somewhere?" Dr. Orlav asked. "I don't know anybody else who is doing research on penguins in this immediate area. Who would need penguins?"

"I don't know," replied Christina, "but it could happen because I think I saw a penguin being carried away in the back of a truck the day you picked us up at the airport. Something was squirming around in a red and blue canvas bag, just like the bag we found at the rookery. So I think someone could be taking penguins somewhere."

If Christina knew a motive for taking penguins, it would certainly help solve the puzzle of the missing penguins! So many questions! She would have to start finding some answers soon! Her visit to the South Pole would be over in just a few days.

"Grant and I will do a little research," Christina told Dr. Orlav.

Dr. Orlav looked puzzled. Grant said, "Don't worry, Dr. Orlav. Christina is the super sleuth. When she starts sniffing after something, she'll find it!"

That evening, Christina and Grant logged onto the Internet. They searched to find any meanings for the words on the note she found in the red and blue bag. Christina typed in the numbers, **77.801 S 166.703 E** but didn't get any results that made sense.

Grant scanned the note again. "Those numbers look familiar." He put his hands on his temples and closed his eyes to concentrate. "I think those numbers are the ones Dr. Orlav gave as our GPS coordinates when we were trapped in the snow!"

"I think you're right!" Christina said, getting excited and clenching her fists. "And another interesting thing—THAT'S precisely where we found the bag with the note!"

Sitting on the table in front of them was a pamphlet describing McMurdo Station. It gave

103

the GPS coordinates for MacTown as 78° S latitude, 168° E longitude. Christina jabbed her finger on the pamphlet and said, "If the expression, "77.801 S 166.703 E" stands for latitude and longitude readings, the spot indicated IS NEAR MacTown. It's probably that magic spot where we found the note!"

Christina then focused back on her Internet search. She typed in the expression, "R-chondrite group," on the search page. Her results were a series of links that looked like Greek to her!

"Nothing about penguins," she sighed. "Just scientists' names, research papers, and types of classification." She then clicked on a link, only to find something about meteorites. "Huh?" Christina said as she looked at the screen. "Still nothing about penguins, but plenty about meteorites."

"Why meteorites?" Grant wondered. "Christina, do you think that bag belonged to one of the scientists studying meteorites?"

"That's a good question, Grant, and it REALLY stumps me," Christina said. She and Grant headed back to their dorm room, deep in thought. Christina picked up the bag. If only there were more clues! She inspected the bag again to see tiny black fragments scattered in the bottom. She shifted the grains in her hand.

"You may be right, Grant," Christina said. "These little specs could be meteorite pieces. A scientist may have been using this pack to carry meteorites. But something bothers me. What about this awful smell?"

"Christina, you are always sniffing around," Grant remarked. He grabbed the bag and took a deep whiff.

He crinkled his nose in disgust.

"Now, doesn't the inside of this bag smell just like penguin poop?" Christina asked.

16

Friend or Foe?

The next day was a busy one at the ranch. Dr. Orlav furiously prepared to bring his missing penguins back to the corral. He said there was a lot of "red tape" involved in getting the birds back. Grant figured that whatever tape Dr. Orlav was talking about naturally had to be red, because everything else was in Antarctica!

Grant was pleased to find no more missing penguins as he completed his morning chores. All twenty were present, even the two from the Club. Christina found another new baby chick. That totaled six, including the two little chicks with sweaters, Shiny and Baldy, who scurried around the corral in comfort. Fred said they were starting to sprout new feathers, and grow taller.

Grant said, "We'll have to change their names to Fluffy and Downy when their feathers come out!"

Christina pulled out her camera to view the first photos of Shiny and Baldy. She wanted to see how the birds had changed since the first pictures were taken. She continued to scroll through the earlier pictures she had taken. When she saw the pictures taken at the newly discovered rookery, something caught her eye. What were the objects in the background of each picture? She needed to enlarge the images on the computer screen later to get a better look.

That evening, Christina told Grant about her discovery in the pictures taken at the rookery. Grant got his camera and scrolled through the images he took at the rookery on the first visit. They transferred the images to their laptops and zoomed in on the objects—clearly visible in both Christina's and Grant's pictures.

Christina mused, "Those are black rocks. They could be nothing more than volcanic rocks, like the ones sticking out of the snow around MacTown. But...I think they look just like the meteorites we saw in Dr. Frieda's presentation."

"They sure do," Grant agreed. "That could explain why we found those black specs of rock in the red and blue bag, and..."

Christina leaped up, interrupting him. "And why the note found in the bag may be giving a meteorite location and classification!"

"Maybe we should go show these images to Dr. Frieda." Grant suggested. "She's the expert on meteorites. She might even be the owner of the bag!"

"In her talk," Christina said, trying to stay calm and think clearly, "Dr. Frieda reported where she and other scientists found meteorites." Christina then rubbed her forehead in an attempt to remember the exact words in the scientist's talk. "I don't think she mentioned this place." She paused and then told Grant, "I wonder IF we CAN talk to Dr. Frieda about this."

"Why do you say that, Christina?" Grant asked, alarmed.

"There HAS to be a reason why this spot wasn't mentioned in her talk," Christina answered in a **canny** way. "Either she doesn't know, or

doesn't want anybody else to know. Considering she IS an expert, it's more likely she does know."

Grant did not want to hear this about a scientist. He shot back, "No, Christina, we can't start thinking she might be up to no good. We don't know her. She could be friend or foe, but we really don't know!"

Crooks in the Rookery

Christina folded her arms across her chest. "So," she said to Grant, "what do we positively know?"

Grant held up one finger. "First, we know that Dr. Orlav's three missing penguins were found at the rookery," he said. Grant held up another finger. "Second, we know we found a bag containing a note giving the rookery location and a meteorite type. And inside the bag we found what looks like meteorite pieces and smells like penguin poop. And last,..." he added, holding up a third finger, "we got notes warning us to not go near penguins."

"That second fact is important," Christina said firmly. "Penguins and meteorites are found in the

same bag and the same location, a location that was pinpointed on the note in the bag!"

"So?" Grant asked, confused.

"If the bag and all the notes we saw did not exist," Christina explained, "I think this would be a case of penguins, on their own, migrating to a natural rookery—which happens to be near a meteorite find. Dr. Orlav gets his penguins back, case closed."

"So we need to ask what the bag and the notes are telling us!" Grant deducted.

"Yes! Let's start with the bag," Christina replied as she held up the red and blue bag. "This looks and smells like it was used to transport penguins AND meteorites. Since I saw a bag that LOOKED like it was being used for transporting penguins, I think I can say this bag was most likely used for that purpose."

"Why?" Grant asked. "Like Dr. Orlav said, who'd want to transport penguins? As you and I know, they are hard to handle!"

"Maybe the person wanted some penguins to be there at that spot," Christina said, her

thoughts racing, "so that no one would go near the spot!"

"Yeah!" Grant said, "No one's supposed to go near a penguin rookery without special permission. But why make that spot off limits?"

"Maybe to hide the fact that valuable meteorites are there!" Christina yelped, clapping her hands. "That WOULD be a good motive to move a few penguins there!"

Grant's eyes widened, now understanding it all. He said, "That's why we got the notes to stay away from penguins!"

Christina agreed. "That person must have known you loved penguins and would be looking out for the birds," she explained. "He or she might have even known you were counting penguins. If so, you would find out something— which is exactly what's happened!"

Grant thought of a new angle. "If someone was moving penguins to a location, they would also want fish or krill to entice the birds to get into the bags."

"That's great, Grant!" Christina praised her brother. "That would account for the missing krill at Dr. Orlav's ranch and the aquarium lab! Now that we have a motive," she concluded, "we can possibly have some suspects—people we've met here who could have sent those warnings to us."

"Dr. Frieda," Grant said, with a sad expression, "is high on the list because she's a meteor expert. She would know how valuable the meteorites are."

"I know she appeared to be a nice person," Christina replied, "but that could be just a **cloying** act to hide her real purposes!"

"Then there are Al Pearson and Brett Brackets," Grant considered. "They have access to trucks, and move all over the place in their work. That Brett seems to know a lot about a lot things. HE might know the value of meteorites."

"That's right," Christina said. "When we were trapped in the ice, Brett volunteered to rescue us because he was in our area."

"Do you suppose he drove the truck we chased?" Grant asked. "That would put him close by, and rescuing us would take suspicion off him!"

"Then there's Fred—or even worse, Dr. Orlav!" Christina cried. "I don't want to even think about that! Fred Freckles couldn't do anything like that, and I don't think a friend of Papa's would either!"

"They definitely have access to the penguins, the trucks, and the meteorite field," Grant replied, sticking with his theory.

"No, no," Christina insisted. "We KNOW them. Besides, they helped us a lot to solve the mystery. They're on our side. We must trust them with our findings. We need their help to catch the culprit or culprits."

The next morning, Christina and Grant showed Dr. Orlav the pictures of the meteorites and all the notes the kids had received. Christina explained the notes, and said, "You see, Dr. Orlav,

your penguins were taken there to keep people away from the meteorite find. Your missing krill was used to entice the penguins."

Dr. Orlav was stunned. "Crooks in the rookery!" he cried. "Who do you think did it?"

Christina listed her suspects, including Fred but not Dr. Orlav, of course.

"It couldn't be Dr. Ortiz," Dr. Orlav observed. "She left Antarctica just after giving her talk. She had a family emergency. I would vouch for Fred. He's first rate. And Al, well, Al has been too busy fixing things to go anywhere or do anything!"

"By process of elimination, that means it must be Brett Brackets!" Christina cried, making the connection between driving a truck and the bagged penguin in the back of the truck. "HE was at the airport, herded penguins, and could have driven the truck with the bagged penguin inside! He could have put the note in our baggage, and dropped that newspaper article in the Hagglund when he rescued us! Also, we actually saw him with a bag of krill at the aquarium! I can't think of a reason why it couldn't be him. Can you?"

Grant and Dr. Orlav shook their heads. "Well," Dr. Orlav said, "we'd better tell your grandparents what's going on, and then call the marshal!"

After speaking to Mimi and Papa, Dr. Orlav called the U.S. marshal, Bill Merrick. On hearing the story, the marshal decided to set a trap. Everyone at McMurdo Station would be told today about the new rookery, but the location would be published tomorrow.

Christina clapped her hands. "That will force the culprit to collect the valuable meteorites before tomorrow!"

"Right! And we can be waiting to catch the troublemaker!" the marshal said.

After the news was broadcast, Dr. Orlav, the marshal, Christina, and Grant staked out the rookery by hiding behind a hill in their Hagglund. Within an hour, a truck arrived at the rookery. A figure, bundled up and unrecognizable, jumped out of the truck and hurried to the meteorite fall. A gust of wind blew back the man's hood as he bent to put some stones in a bag. "Oh, my gosh!" Christina whispered. "It's Brett Bracketts taking the forbidden meteorites!"

The marshal ran out and grabbed a startled Brett. "Get here early, did you, to grab the meteorites before anyone else knew what was here?" he asked.

Grant piped up, "And did you take Dr. Orlav's penguins and bring them here?"

Brett just stammered in shock and surprise.

After questioning, Brett explained, "This is a real rookery. I just wanted to enlarge it for a while to keep people away from the meteorites." He admitted to removing meteorites from the site and bringing penguins to the site.

With Christina and Grant giving him angry looks, Brett said sheepishly, "I didn't 'borrow' THAT many penguins! I WAS going to return them."

Christina crossed her arms across her chest. "Yeah, and I bet you took the krill and wrote us those notes to stay away from penguins, too!"

Brett nodded his head in embarrassment as the marshal handcuffed him.

18

On Top of the World

Dr. Orlav said that solving this mystery called for another celebration to thank Christina and Grant. Grant suggested, "If you're going to have a party for us, we want to invite all the penguins, and welcome the missing penguins back to the ranch!"

Dr. Orlav laughed and said, "That could be arranged. I'll have Fred take care of the details. How about tomorrow at the ranch? And, please invite anybody you want!"

The next day, an "Ivan the Terra" bus carried all the guests to Dr. Orlav's penguin ranch. Christina, Grant, Mimi, and Papa invited Dr. Frieda, who had just returned from emergency

leave. They also asked Al Pearson and many others, even Dr. Grouchy Pants, to join the party.

The bus rumbled into the ranch. Dr. Orlav greeted his guests and brought them into a shed decorated with red, blue, and yellow balloons. Streamers of the same colors hung from the rafters. A sign with huge red letters said, "Thanks to Christina and Grant, All Penguins Are Back Safe and Sound!"

When everyone was seated, Dr. Orlav thanked Christina and Grant for finding his missing penguins, and for detecting a serious crime in Antarctica—the theft of meteorites. Dr. Orlav then described how Brett Brackets wanted the meteorites for himself because they could be used to make very expensive jewelry!

In a shy voice, Grant asked, "Where are the penguins? Was there too much red tape to bring them to the party?"

Dr. Orlav laughed, twirled his mustache, and called out, "Open, sesame!"

Fred yanked open a sliding door behind the crowd. There on the ice outside, a bright red carpet led from a parked truck to the door. Fred

opened the rear door of the truck, and out jumped all the ranch penguins, including Baldy, Shiny, and the missing birds. Everyone, even Dr. Grouchy Pants, yelled,

"Hurray! Hip, Hip Hurray!"

The penguins, with The General in the lead, waddled along the red carpet, ready to join the party. Grant ran over to Dr. Orlav, squeezed him

121

in a bear hug, and said, "This is just the best day ever! Even though I'm at the bottom of the world, I feel like I'm on the top of the world!"

THE END

About the Author

Carole Marsh is an author and publisher who has written many works of fiction and non-fiction for young readers. She travels throughout the United States and around the world to research her books. In 1979 Carole Marsh was named Communicator of the Year for her corporate communications work with major national and international corporations.

Marsh is the founder and CEO of Gallopade International, established in 1979. Today, Gallopade International is widely recognized as a leading source of educational materials for every state and many countries. Marsh and Gallopade were recipients of the 2004 Teachers' Choice Award. Marsh has written more than 50 Carole Marsh Mysteries™. In 2007, she was named Georgia Author of the Year. Years ago, her children, Michele and Michael, were the original characters in her mystery books. Today, they continue the Carole Marsh Books tradition by working at Gallopade. By adding grandchildren Grant and Christina as new mystery characters, she has continued the tradition for a third generation.

Ms. Marsh welcomes correspondence from her readers. You can e-mail her at fanclub@gallopade.com, visit carolemarshmysteries.com, or write to her in care of Gallopade International, P.O. Box 2779, Peachtree City, Georgia, 30269 USA.

Built-In Book Club
Talk About It!

1. Why were the scientists so upset about Grant having a cold? What are some things Grant could do to avoid spreading his cold to others?

2. Do you prefer cold weather or hot weather? Why?

3. Grant just loves penguins! Most people find them very interesting. Why do you think that is? What would you like to know about penguins?

4. What do you think it would be like to live in a place where it is daylight all the time in the "austral summer?" Would you like it, or would you dislike it?

5. Do you like to eat "freshies?" If so, what are some of your favorite "freshies?"

6. Grant and Christina did a good job of counting their penguins. Why was it a good idea to keep a close count on the penguins at the ranch?

7. Why is it so difficult for people to live in Antarctica? Why was it so difficult for explorers to reach the South Pole?

8. There were scientists from many countries at McMurdo Station. What is good about meeting people from other nations?

9. Were you surprised to find out why the penguins were missing? Do you think the "bad guy" had a pretty smart plan?

10. Would you like to travel to Antarctica someday? Why or why not?

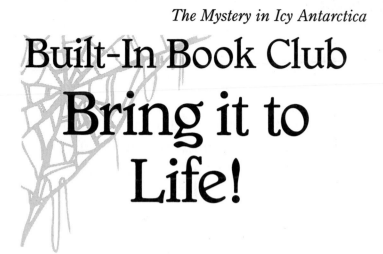

Built-In Book Club
Bring it to Life!

1. **Map It!** Find a map of Antarctica—it's at the bottom of the world! Take a piece of poster board and draw a map of Antarctica. Label the oceans around it. Add some icebergs! Draw some whales and Weddell seals in the water near the continent. Which continent is closest to Antarctica?

2. **Bundle Up!** What would you need to keep warm in Antarctica? Make a list of what you would need to wear to keep warm in such a cold

place. Start at your head and go down to your toes! What are some warm things you like to eat? List those, too. Share your list with other club members. (Who likes chicken noodle soup, besides me???)

3. **Make It!** Create a penguin bookmark! You will need stiff white construction paper, glue, and a Popsicle® stick. First, draw your penguin. Color it (don't forget cute little orange feet!), and cut it out. Next, glue the bottom of your penguin to the top of your Popsicle stick. To use, place the Popsicle stick between your book pages and let the penguin keep your place!

4. **Keep the Peace!** Did you know that there is an Antarctic Treaty? More than 40 countries have signed this agreement. The member nations have agreed to preserve the continent of Antarctica for science. Research the treaty on the Internet and list all the nations who have signed this important treaty. Use a piece of poster board to list them, and draw each country's flag next to its name. Color the flags.

Antarctica Trivia

1. Antarctica is the coldest and windiest continent on the earth!

2. A sheet of ice almost a mile thick covers almost all of Antarctica. In fact, Antarctica doubles in size in the winter because of the ice that forms along the coastline!

3. One of the biggest icebergs ever recorded broke from the Ross Ice Shelf in Antarctica in 2000. It was about the size of Connecticut!

4. The Antarctic Convergence is a zone in the ocean around Antarctica where cold water meets warmer water from the north. Tiny, shrimp-like creatures known as krill thrive there, attracting whales to a krill feast!

5. During feeding season, an adult blue whale can eat about 4 million krill per day!

6. The Antarctic ice cap holds between 60 and 70 percent of the world's fresh water.

7. Scientists regularly drill deep into the Antarctic ice and remove "ice cores." These cylinders of ice provide valuable information about the earth's climate in the past.

8. Penguins have oily, waterproof feathers and a thick layer of fat for insulation.

9. Unlike other birds, penguins have solid bones. These bones add weight, helping them dive into the water for food.

10. There are no trees or bushes in Antarctica. The only vegetation includes lichens, mosses, and algae.

Glossary

adamant: determined, unshakeable

allocate: distribute, or set aside for a special purpose

austral: south, pertaining to or coming from the south

benevolent: kind, intending good will

canny: shrewd, careful

cloying: unappealing, overwhelming sweetness

fingy: a newcomer to the South Pole

Hagglund: a personnel carrier on treads that is commonly used in Antarctica

ice floe: a large piece of ice floating on a body of water

rookery: a breeding ground for birds

skidoo: a snowmobile used in Antarctica

snotsicles: a real word used by Australians living at the South Pole; it refers to the streams of frozen mucus that form from a runny nose

stake out: to watch a place over a period of time from a hidden place

Scavenger Hunt

Want to have some fun? Let's go on a scavenger hunt! See if you can find the items below related to the mystery. *(Teachers: you have permission to reproduce this page.)*

1. _____ an ice cube tray

2. _____ a red winter jacket

3. _____ a picture of a Hagglund

4. _____ some long underwear

5. _____ a ping-pong ball

6. _____ a stuffed penguin toy

7. _____ a broom (to sweep up
penquin droppings!)

8. _____ a carrot
(your favorite freshie?)

9. _____ a yellow sweater
(like Baldy's!)

10. _____ a dab of red paint on a piece
of paper

Visit the <u>carolemarshmysteries.com</u> website to:

- Join the Carole Marsh Mysteries™ Fan Club!

- Write a letter to Christina, Grant, Mimi, or Papa!

- Cast your vote for where the next mystery should take place!

- Find fascinating facts about the countries where the mysteries take place!

- Track your reading on an international map!

- Take the Fact or Fiction online quiz!

- Find out where the *Mystery Girl* is flying next!